THE MANY WOODS OF GRIEF

DATE DUE

FEB 1 0 2012

THE MANY WOODS OF GRIEF
Poems

Lucas Farrell

UNIVERSITY OF MASSACHUSETTS PRESS
Amherst and Boston

LC 201100337
ISBN 978-1-55849-899-0

Designed by Sally Nichols
Set in Didot
Printed and bound by BookMobile, Inc.

Library of Congress Cataloging-in-Publication Data

Farrell, Lucas.
The many woods of grief : poems / Lucas Farrell.
    p. cm.
ISBN 978-1-55849-899-0 (pbk. : alk. paper)
I. Title.
PS3606.A7355M36 2011
811'.6 – dc22

                                        201100337

British Library Cataloguing in Publication data are available.

for my parents

CONTENTS

THE MANY WOODS OF GRIEF

WE ARE ALL OF US NEARLY HOME

In the furious meadow, each
blowing leaf a tiny calendar.
What time was it, what year.
I have loved her how long.
A green darkness traces patterns
through grass,
reciting the reasons why flowers
appear black in old movies. Over here
I see the sun has found religion.
He is up to his waist
in Floridian rye.
According to the flaking,
splotchy red of my knuckles,
we have everything to fear.
Which is why the horseflies mistake us
for beggars. And why passions multiply
in the country by four-fifths,
which I finally agree is sufficient.
For the sun here is an epileptic.
Is someone you love
in the midst of a fit.
I'm asking you to feel deep weight,
intolerable helplessness.
The earth is spinning the way children might
when a storm overhead
performs its invitational curtsy.
For the stars we've issued arrest warrants.
The blackness between them
has been shaped into badges.
The nosy offenders surrender
like snow geese. All birds
are authentic at night. We are
all of us nearly home,

explains the beggar.
Explains the tiny calendar.
Not now.
I'm trying to describe to you the weather.

I

GRAFFITI

I am told that branches, once grafted,
will sing again, as was once,
they were willing to tell, this story
& I, a mere passerby, was told it.

My cell makes mute a youthful tone,
but I am not one to be trusted.
I have been incarcerated
for better things than you and she.

There is a crack, many, a forehead
and when that happens, you can't
expect love to find shape, formless
as the sea, the alphabet of graffiti.

I am most unlike an arrow,
or a progressing arrow, or a paragram
in the middle of a tortoise shell,
the keystone shape of myth.

I have not forgotten the words,
I have not, I have not forgot.
I have forgotten not, nor
have I, as it sounds, ever

& that is exactly where I stand,
never an inch, never any inch
closer to the next half-way point
where the tradition, the brick &

sea, engage in pageantry.
I was once in love with her,
her mouth wide on my wall,
drawn there as if I could almost speak.

GEOSMIN

When I speak and nothing happens,
nothing changes, my very very bird.
My mnemonic sweat laps the window slats
in the dream of another's making.
Place your forehead against my forehead and we'll
see who sweats first. Unintentional separation. The tongue
of memory licks my ear, takes some version of forever
to dry. You are a tall tree, a feathery tree, my very very tree.
Your leaves are fly swatters. Half baby blue, half navy blue,
the sky rushes in. Old skiff, run ashore and stripped,
has been designed to fit the mind's jalousie windows.
We play Throats & Chimes in the parlor
over expensive cubes of ice.
Irreparably, you belong here, in this cool
below. Admiring your velvety roots, I tell myself
I own my toe's wiggle, can see it tingle right there
in front of me. Pulsing white oval kisses. Oh, your bucket
of warm water, with its splash of vinegar!
You wipe the windows obsessively, increasing
your *schein*. I sink deeper into my wooden chair,
which gives and gives the way suspicions do.
The wooden screws replaced by metal in the name of permanence.
So it will never come apart again, so never again apart it will come.
Out the window, the dark earth has been eviscerated
by worms never touched by the hands of children.
Carefully, I listen for it: endless patience, melts away.
The bird buried alive
during a heavy rain, a cartilage rain,
the inexorable wings.

THE LAST ARCTIC

1

My mother calls me Luna Moth.
She says I will dust the far-end perches.
When I lie in bed
with the lights off she brushes
my teeth & they are hers.
In the silencing wind of the poplar farm
she contorts her mouth into pale
geographic compositions.
Weathervane, deep well,
static gestures, a time quarry
whose spoils replace my molars, we are
of God's netted inhale.
My father sighs, standing on the porch, arms
folded to his chest. One cuticle
of moonlight constricts, scrapes
across his lip, audible, not like a father moth
but aching spoken swollen
in the earth.
But when I flap my wings, encircle her,
rub my sweet gum against her wrist,
she tastes like dark night.
Like warm patient stars.

2

I sleep in the pit now.
He has taken me away from her.
I dream of her breath polishing
a green apple like an off-air
weather channel.
There are others now.
They stand like scarecrows,

hind wings unfurling into jagged breeze puzzles.
They let their eyes dry.
Watch the blur bend
& become my astronomy.
I crease & soil garments though I'm naked.
In the dark they hear me gnaw the trough
until my jaw unleashes the cold night air.
Sometimes I talk to roots
& the roots keep the sound in the sky
from pouring down.

3

I think we make the scarecrows insecure.
I am hurting myself.
I arch my back against the slope
of terrain & without ribs I think.
It isn't wet now. Green heat echoes up
& down these fields at night,
drizzling meal in the hedges, the molars
& jaw click.
The stars in their sky-well
swivel in pulse.
Like boiling, breaching beets.

FINGERS POINT AT THE NEW MOON RISING

It was early evening.
I knew no one.
Everyone knew her.
We knocked on the door.
They were not projected home. They were
home. She struck a deal with each
of them, we crossed a creek, I felt alone,
a creek we had crossed before. Caddis husks
in a tin can. The sun was starving, mute
black. We led ourselves to the door:
we were in a valley, plugging our eyes
with ointment. We were capable
and lathered. There was buzzing
in the bulrush, apostate sky (the migrating ones
were good and gone). I held the meadowlark
thrashing, tight as I could. I thrust it against her
breast. The sky was a jet stream. It burst
through seams of feathered flesh,
a drinking fountain, ice cold, plugged-in,
insects. We shut our eyes
and listened. Wind in the grass.

STITCHES

The bird fell from the sky.
Let me be clear: The bird.
It fell from the sky.
And I was the first to discover
it there. I happened to have
a razor because I was told
I should shave. Instead, I
sliced the torso and sniffed.
I sliced the torso with a razor
and pinched the heart to see
if it would flap like a fish
and carve my wrist with its scales.
It smelled like a fish.
A bird smells like a fish.
And I was relieved because
I had long thought it true.
I said to them, listen.
Let me be clear:
The scales will slice my
wrist, that's why I want gloves
you fucking asshole hicks.
It's not that I am a girl.
I am not. It's just that,
do you want me to smell
like that. I will smell
like a fish. And you wonder,
you wonder why I don't shave.
Do fish shave. Do birds.
Do birds shave. Answer me.
What do you have
to say. Here it is.
It fell from the sky.

GENERATION OF BIRD

The generations of the bird are all
By water washed away. They follow after.
They follow, follow, follow, in water washed away.
            Wallace Stevens, "Somnambulisma"

There is a directness of tilt, a subtle knock, and behind
the door a face exposed to a face that is not ours. We are
gesture and therefore hopeful. This face, this facelessness, is
not the source of anxiety but it is a world and therefore. But
the composer sees the way string itself unravels and it might
be a bug and there's certainly some crawling and, as a result,
hesitation. Our first act is to keep the eyes a moment shut.
Her eyes are not shut but there is a blinking which is just
to say time is of some importance and what awkwardness, to
blink out loud like that. Speak to the first person we see upon
opening our eyes.

A wooden fence on the bank of a drying creek flow. A quilt unfurled, an imprint of each shared dream. A cross plank christens slump, fallen at an angle that angle is 17. Descending the hill, in the distance, the girl scooches us over. This is the line. Whether imaginary or not it won't budge. There is an angle of the hill and an angle of the fence. From above the creek, below the surface of the water, her face opens. Crossing the line, we awaken inside a throat.

Seats cave us toward the center, the angle of below. We knead some physics. Foreheads furrow and the girl appears to stammer. Who among us arrives aware. Ushers guide us through aisles, by our wrists. To blink is to shut the eyes. Compose again. Hope tectonics. This is vision this is precipice this is the wondrous longing of posture.

In the exhibit hall of throat, an apostrophic leaf. It freezes on a stair. The verb *to freeze* has an angle 1 where now it is clearly 2. No make-up no genre no contextual glue. What it has is our attention. We fall to fall in love.

Welcome, my love, to the theater of shin splints.

Later there is an angle that angle is 4. A hallway without the doors. We lose ourselves, cave of sense-compliance. What is light if not disclosed through a rumor of gray-black glow. There is a handprint around the neck—is it proof of osmotic screen. An alphabet in one hand, in the other oceanic seams.

Palpable pulse (one two one two), the cinematics of pursuit.

Heretofore we know her soft skin as if we were a razor and she never makes a sound. That silence is the sea, the seashell. The slicing has an angle, that angle is 3. It is also an act. In its ancient roots, film is nickname is romance is emulsive blood dispersal. Is land where there is no land.

She presses her finger to the pit, where ash is white and cloud-forms dry. A print: the more she is the less it stings the present. The stinging has an angle. She has addressed it many times. The numbers she recites. The angle is math is mute is what makes her in the night. What darkness struggles back to the screen.

SAD TOPOLOGY OF A B-MOVIE LOVE TRYST

On certain days, I glimpse
the shadow of my profile
on the hull of the boat
and I want my lips
to leave me alone,
I want my lips alone
in a room, cleaved
by night-light, a glass box
of dinoflagellates,
a spray of what was said
when you saw me,
peripherally,
pounding promises
into the heroine,
the story unclothed,
blaring glove of radiance,
where I dreamed
of rescuing
a made-up she who needed
rescuing,
and the light plugged
into the wrong wall
in the wrong room,
flickers and goes
out, deeper down
than out,
and he who was
not in the room,
he whose shadow
was not on the wall,
lips not turned out,
folded into the dark
like the shaping of

a kiss, the armed ship
of a retina,
splash of
stars on seafloor,
which is enough
in this day and age
to agitate the surface,
enough to become,
in a dark room,
in the glowing letters,
in a lover's room
full of loving stories,
more than itself.

CRABGRASS

It pains me that I whisper
softly, that each morning the driveway
smells of dusk, that I can't seem to
wash the filth off my gums.
I've learned to wait patiently,
flora and neutrinos
relax my restless routine.
Inch-by-inch they enter in,
my tangled six-pronged heart.
I'll sit for hours daydreaming,
waiting for you to arrive at the fencepost,
sweat-pants stemmed,
white petal hands, dripping dew
between the legs I demand,
as I've always done, to come and soothe
my tongue.

I sometimes squint my eyes.
I'd rather not trim the yard, strip
the steps, pour the moon's sweet milk
into my calloused hands,
spilling like silt on ocean
floors or crustal summits, depending
on your scientific stance.
I think we'd all agree:
perspective varies lonesomely.
I make irrational statements.
I steal the beauty from the flowers.
I should be cut down before I take up
any more space in this world.
If I knew your inclinations, perhaps
I'd take you down with me.
I say this because it makes it

easier come summer, when
my polymeric soul rises up
at last and makes a pass
at death. Come play,
as I kneel on all fours.
Snipping
away at strangers I often mistake
for myself.

THE ACCORDIONIST

My sister stole my pulse
& sold it for a slide,
a metal one, a gaudy one,
a get-yourself-swept-away-by-one
kind of one,
a down
& around &
in & out
kind of love.
I *love* my sister,
she's
frustratingly
earnest &
full of hatred
& I want her
to be happy always
& a little bit sad
like our mother,
who's a grassy place
behind the trailers.
She lies there
under ground
& whistles,
blowing bubbles
that sound
like stars in rough winds,
like cardboard spines
squished between
arthritic
hands, knuckles
where they shouldn't
be, red & swollen,
a mess of tongues

in the compost
pile, wagging.
Making a wish
doesn't require a voice.
Like how to imply
goodbye
mechanically,
fanatically,
a factory, a poplar farm,
a paper mill
punched in the face
by a living, filmy thing
that's moving quickly
away, going quickly
& thoughtfully
away.

YOU WHO TAUGHT YOURSELF BRAILLE

I will not let you break my man-heart, not today.
The traffic is charming, rustling—
my neighbor blows on ivy tendrils lodged
in the brick wall, telling them, *shame on you.*
I'm finding myself unable to eat lunch.
I stand all day in front of a mirror and pirouette,
searching for new moles. I never realized I had moles,
now I have thousands, I have millions. If you
keep a bee trapped in a jar for a day and watch it.
If you're patient. If you remove the top and it's
a Thursday, and you place it on the table. No joke,
the bee will remain in the open jar until you leave
the room. If you were blind, I'd let you rub
your hands all over me. I'd ask, *what does it say?*

THE DUAL-SHADE OF SIX-PRONG

***

Literally, I combed the desert,
traded grass for movie-lines,
a generation in myself:

the dual-shade of six-prong

—the molecular structure
of perspicuous love.

Somewhere in the middle
the words
got stuck, unplugged,
electric blood
poured
& the wind,

the ecstatic math-wind:

Deep God, on the in-spoke.

I combed the curls,
the still-frill of cursive-scalp,
& smeared charcoal dust
in sculpted
letters,

air.
No, that was a peat bog.
No, that was a graveyard.

You wrote, I've been sweating
in temples for centuries

& what's it
got me? Some fire-
robe to perform a rain

dance in?

My knees are scrub-bone-gray
& there's a dual-shade
where my
eyelids stray. It's windy,

here.
Therefore, grass for movie-lines
(fracture, scripture).
Friction of lyric's cellular lure—
flatliner green.

Focus on the projected stitch-seam.
My God-given name.

***

sure my parts
come
in a box

all packaged

with hands
tiny faces carved

into them sure
it's aflame

blackening

rust

then rusting

don't we all

don't tell me
it's a lie

don't
you tell me
with your

eyes

closed I'm a
liar

open
them

***

A migratory bird masters the dial tone.
Language of the electrical socket, the outlet.
                    Thereby granting
flicker, groove to sprocket,

                              steady:

My refrigerator light makes its way toward you.
The cookiecutter shark makes its way toward you.

Albeit your source is depleted:

albeit my apostrophe is the death of a star
journeying toward the last of your say

uprooted, in transit, dual-shade—

our limits
graze

***

The river's
knees are swollen
like walking
me to sleep

every night

I can't tell you how
sorry the sun looks
this morning
through its

trampled
silkscreen
face

I will
inject and pump myself into

where I oughtn't
be

capable of
weathering loudly,

effluent

superstitiously red,

left
superstitiously red

pouring down
my two-
dimensional

shins,

plumbing the dark
spots
of my cartoon

trees

***

If you can conceive of a river,
rare, unclean,
how many times we'll rush the sea.

Fear is worse than it was before.
We know less about dying.
No rituals, no lore.

Dad worked the paper mill.
Beds stripped of sheets,
my brothers & me with static eyes.

It wasn't lightning tore us up.
We bare-kicked blankets,

electrified dust.

The end of elegy was an oil swirl,
colors unknown.

It was the thaw

told us: grow,
in the timeless way.
When the ink melted
into eye patches

on parking lots,
& the moon became a skinless grape,
& stars became
our mother's words,

did we speak of the end?
The dead in books shook
leaves & laughed when

the trees bent out of shape.
Conveyer belt jams
preserved the night.

***

      Say:
I forgot where it was I was born.
There was migration in
the epigraph, a dam
in the form.

The bedtime stories were:

Let the torment outlast
the fossil fuels of happiness.

***

When you came along
each prong received
a slightly different charge.
Infinitesimal,
my six-pronged heart.

           My salmonfly hatch,
           my arctic tern,
           my silver poplar,
           my elephant seal, my windmill,
                my troubled teeth.

You blew through your milky green siphon
& called the rain
that fell on me

           janitor-rain
because I once was

scrub & jukebox
& there would be nothing left to clean up
when our fire was through.

Not to mention your heart
all lit up like a bug zapper—

      you who once knew how to light
on a stray wrist, in the rain, in the dark.

You looked right at me.

II

LOGIC OF RAWHIDE

You close your eyes
and plunge a fist,
irrationalize a ripple.
You squeeze tight,

keep the coin dry.
She said she'd never
leave you. Sweet
as honeysuckle

in a cobble dream.

You played cards
through the rain.
The silly wishing well
game. There's your

water proof, she said.
Shook the rawhide
from her head.

Later, you slept with
your tongue stuck
to her thigh.

Bit of early summer
rain-rise.

The wing flutter
drips a mating call flash
long after the finger

smash. Crescents
applied under eyes

to keep
from sleeping,
you can't lose her
now. Incandescent
swell from deep

down the nerve-well.

So you took the
harness to her.
Attached her to the tree,
till salt pressed

stiff the shagbark
leaves.

You traced a circle
around that on horseback.
You held it steady,
through the night

and all the next day.

For three straight days.
Then you reached
the insect phase,

the kind that scar the brain.

She glowed like sapphire,
like worm sweat.
You sliced

the horse's eyes
with a thumbnail.

White blood
went like blackbirds
in the night.
You held on tight

and let her bearings
form.
What needed you
now, you hushed it
with your hand,

spoke to it soft,
whispered steady,
voice sturdy

as a rich man
in a suit, in a rain.

REGARDING RAIN

\Myth One\

It was the year the rain went dry,
kept falling, day in day out,
for there was no
precedence of dust.

Dust was rain, phlegm in season,
vocabulary sparse, a shift.

At that instant, we all got wet
and felt wet.
It was not the last time, of course.
But it was the first.

\Myth Two\

The puddle never dried, its function
a debate, some for and some against,
vehemently soaked, our throats
slid. The elders tried to fire it.
Fathom this:
a flame for water.

\Myth Three\

A variation of the rain dance,
ceremonial in its seriousness,
there was fissure/chasm,
a real need for stitch-work.
The youth learned
touch, touched and danced.
It was nice to feel the rain.

\Myth Four\

How the story got passed along
is another story; and in that story
was a linen room,
where voice made shift
a silent press. It was warm,
got warmer, as the earth bumped
up against more earth.

\Myth Five\

In geologic
time, we question it and listen
for it all our lives.
There are answers and there
is some great need for them.
There is often a fingertip that meets
another, and in between some pinch
of rain.

\Myth Six\

There was another finger
touched
the puddle in the rain.
It traced some lick of thirst,
a word that is a word,
discovered a wave that sunk
the earth. This is not what it
means to feel the rain.

\Myth Seven\

In the time
of a human life,
where deserts become us
and stiff the breath.
There is a question under breath,
tongue and under mouth.
There is some need to regard it.
A regarding and some regard for
the ancient crustal vacant vein.

TO THE VISIONARY

Make of your blind spots a Braille strip.
Now touch yourself. Now witness the coffee
never grow cold. Defying entropy
this morning feels good.
Sitting on this lawn feels good. In this,
the shiest angle of light.
The blacksmith's
fire-poking of shadow.
Your Braille strip I gift to the sparrows,
coat hooks, they hang themselves in turn.
Too black, I'm afraid, for your liking.
Too early in the morning for thrill.
Forgive me if the coffee brands stars to your tongue.
I haven't wept in years.

TRANSLATIONS OF "MY REFRIGERATOR LIGHT MAKES ITS WAY TOWARD YOU" INTO THE 34 LANGUAGES SPOKEN IN THE MANY WOODS OF GRIEF

> *If man was indeed born when the first animal wept, then it should be*
> *clear enough why I have been dying to drown.*
> —*River of Life*

***

If it weren't for my refrigerator light
I'd acknowledge the incandescence of the bird in my refrigerator,
the one I understand to be a regular bird, just a regular old bird
without a head.

***

I'm afraid God thinks I'm his telephone voice.

***

I'm afraid God thinks I'm his nose in profile.

***

I'm afraid if God saw me, he would very nearly recognize me.
Lost as he would be in my many woods of grief.

***

Don't touch my things,
he would want to say—

so say it.

***

Welcome to the three-star
hotel of my mind.

***

Like anyone else,
I quote the many woods of grief.

***

For instance, the moon here is divided into thirds.

***

The moon is a love triangle dropped in a flour bin
(its white cloud outpour incorrigible, soft).

***

Months come and go as if bearing
fresh trout for supper.

***

You, me, our awesome appliances.

***

I'd like to use that toothbrush, please,
the one with your face attached.

***

In the orchard of beloved green apples,
there is a relinquishing of the city-body, the city-self.

***

My refrigerator light is one weir in the River.

***

Like the flesh of a stranger's elbow
in the backseat of your mother's fears,
wait for it (my refrigerator light)
to brush up against you.

***

You whose seawater floods my acoustic guitar.

***

In the same way bees dodge raindrops in the night,
given their capacity for discerning particular
shades of black, I've spent
a lifetime searching for the darkest frame of film,
exploring every public archive
in the many woods of grief.

***

This country of *I know what you left unsaid*
as my refrigerator light makes its way toward you.

***

The dial-tone
equivalent to
my unfamiliarity
with aspects of myself.

***

All that is clear is that everyone around here drinks
so as to employ the vocabulary of the birds
we've hunted to extinction
in the many woods of grief.

***

I am fortunate in that I happen to be
a pretty good-looking dead thing.

***

For instance, I could never imagine what it
must feel like to be asphalt in its infancy.

***

When the doctor asked me to have a little faith,
I told her to expose her right breast
so I'd have something to press my unholy against.

***

That's a line should be FedExed to the many woods of grief.

***

Your words are the house lights coming on
after a double-bill screening
in a theatre I was led to ungently by the wrist—
the words whose sole effect
is reaffirming how real this world we live in
must be to live in.

***

No one is ever so alone as in the moment he asks for
the check and receives an incandescent bird
where the dinner mint should be.

***

This is not a precise enough translation
of what I was unable to tell you
the night you became something other
than moonlight in a drawer.

***

I want to and do believe in bird and in you.

BIOGRAPHY OF CREEK

And since I love you
I seek woodpiles,
an ax, blessings from mothers
with chapped hands like steeples.
I am undesirable, like,
I want to hurt you.
There is a chair on which you sit, rain bucket.
And I bathe you.
A wallpaper of famous faces,
hindquarters, domestic surprises.
I garnish all your limbs with arugula
and pink mellifluous oysters.
I offer apophasis, then cripple the table
of show-me-your-cards
you-cheating-sonuvabitch.
And since you love me too,
the ice cubes won't unloose my eyes
for what's-her-face.
Spiders won't limp down my spine
hip-checking the railings of dream piers.
Endearments like scissored rain,
the timberline won't swell.
As if I love because I was born with mouth ajar.
As if a jar in Tennessee.

HER HUNGER, BAROMETRICAL

Meaning, I wore my feathers into the shower
this morning. Meaning, my towels need
washing again. I'm itchy all over.
The coffee's so cold I'm offended. I can't do this.
I shed another layer—
to the bones, rattling tongue depressors,
wind chimes, lips gone numb.
I am on the patio
with my neighbor's wife asking her to scratch my arm,
pointing at the horizon, the coming storm,
not there, there. I am more predictable
than I used to be,
meaning:
I'll clothesline my hands,
meaning: I hungered evenly
the view from up here.

WHENSOEVER IT SNOWS, MY VERMONT

***

For as we look out the window
with fingernails taped to our wrists,
we sense, of anxiety, a persistence.
And last night I dreamed of an audience,
and last night the dead child was it—
the silent film in which you dipped a finger
in the wet of the dead child's eye.
And the grand drape was that shade of red
that we agreed is the shade implicit
behind an eyelid exposed to sun.
Whensoever it snows, my Vermont,
offer up what is neither yours nor mine:
a silent film star
walking down a city street, thinking
of a country road.
For you have dreamed of a country road.
As I have dreamed of a country road.
And the snow I dreamed rendered what's left
of my TV reception—my televised
heart near the bed. Made of what's left
an unfinished bridge—
the singular glow of my better half.
I'm Saigon for a better half, snow-lonesome
for a singular whole.
Whensoever it snows, my Vermont,
my silent film falls in with your slapstick.
And I fall for your silent h's, the waters
that rise and swirl.
Jar of your quietest phrasings.

***

Back into bed for only a minute.
For hardly a minute passes,
and the man again rises up,
retrieves his watch from the TV box.
Of significance is that he leaves.
Of significance is that he returns,
only this time it's for the wallet. And this time
the girl is dressed, applying make-up
at the vanity mirror.
The wallet and what's left of reception.
And last night I dreamed I kissed you goodbye,
and you gestured for me to stay.
And the girl in the film mouths, *Wait just a second.*
In a second I'll join you, we'll go.
And from outside the window, the film star's impatience,
and in it, the girl delights.
And we find ourselves back on the street
where that kind of red implicit
behind an eyelid exposed to the sun
exists in the close-up of lipstick,
in your systematic approach to slapstick,
in the film star's final breaking
of stride.
You are mouthing something forgotten.
Whensoever it snows, my Vermont.

CONVERSATION

Two golden eagles collide in the sky:
lottery balls spinning,
chromosomes clicking.
Feathers' slow waltz, fortune's
fast descent.
This is how relationships evolve:
in freefall, and suddenly I have
difficulty remembering
if wet matches, once dry,
will strike on any of our surfaces.
When I blink,
I cannot see past your lower-case words,
and when I blink, the birds diverge
just in time.
Wings outstretched, they intersect
the last telephone poles.
It's the wings
that stitch horizons
to immediate skies, now that the wire
has been spooled and hauled away.
Once we agreed it was more beautiful this way.

BY WAY OF APOLOGY,

a mountain steps out
from the ordinary.
Visual capillary,
and the birds get on with it.
What is pure is the binge
drinking sky's encounter
with these:
the tern's blistered
exhale,
my Atlantic heap of IOUs.
Because I do.
Because
there isn't
such a thing as a gift
anymore
says the grasshopper
set aflame
yrs ago
by the twelve-yr old.
Go ahead and make
what is there
disappear
like the carvings
in the tongue
of my mother,
the little boozehound.
My rightful watershed.
I feel paralyzed
by the plastic shovel
in the plastic bucket
as it teases
the final thrust
out the is.

I am waiting for it,
saying, look: here I am,
I'm in the grass,
I'm in the country.
Can you find me.

MY MOTHER'S QUICKENED HEART
(Leonid Shower, 2000)

The moon winked on me like I
was his daughter's handsome friend
who might one day make love to another
of his daughter's handsome friends.
I wouldn't, *I want*
my wink back wouldn't.
A cloud slides past the moon
lampshade smooth.
A blind child's eye, my magnifying glass.
She told me what ignites on the inside is as blue
& real as what doesn't. When I first came upon her
sleeping in tall timothy, my wanting to
tie a kite string around her neck
made the wind pick up. No,
made the wind. I determined her age,
gauged the slight of her Formica wrists.
She had 31 years for a while now.
Her thighs were like canoes banging about
rocky streams, were like banging
about at the end of summer.
Her eyelids were iceboxes full of blood-limes.
She was waiting for something,
had been waiting for someone.
It was hot inside the air out here,
grasshoppers covered in red.
I missed my mother. Deep God, I did.
My Deep,
I whispered to the girl's candy cane wrists (she was dying,
pretty thing, she was dead) —
& now the gypsy moon licked the prairie white —
take a chugaluglug. I said,
Do a kkkwwwwkk-sppphhhhooo,

a spooey,
hiss with a steaming iron-tongue,
press the folds
like the moon did, like I'm about to do
for you and for the waters we could have navigated
in our shiny canoe.
Mother, I swear, you're the prettiest thing I ever
and I promise there will be
a most urgent display of camaraderie among the stars tonight.

THE POINTILLISTS

Tonight's many woods have the group of us—
uncoiled meadow-raster—lying flat
in long grass, in alumina sleepwear,
winter-sighing by the twos and threes.
Internal calligraphies—
disassembled, transported, reassembled:
exhalia.
If our voice was geothermal—
if our Braille-birds, generational—
pastoral rictus—
then the train dragging its weight
down our tracks—aching saboteur
of fact—would have fancied the form
its destination would take.
It was robbery and then it wasn't.
Dream's slant rhyme persists with its coal-cars
of orchids, sloshing high mountain rains,
telling us—promising—
Baby, it's all in your head:
America's final, romantic hither.
Tonight's many woods have us thinking we're
the asterism that denies perspective,
distends metaphor, dissolves harmony.
Whereupon,
through our exquisite lorgnette—
the anaphora of star.

THE COOKIECUTTER SHARK
(Isistius Brasiliensis)

1

The seagull in flight dim-lit from below.
The ocean's surface dim-lit from below.
The cookiecutter shark dim-lit from below.

Until all, from below, theaters into one.

The predator's vision learns the survival of *swim*.
Competing with breath toward vast open-air,
rods and cones pumping, their panicked sea-quest—

the ideogram of having-been's longer-lived scrim,
the soluble silhouette, the very dim ever-traced.
Projected on the screen the light to be consumed,

but the cookiecutter shark preys on the myopic,
actively reads the projectionists' habits,
knows all the lines of their favorite films,

       until all, from above, fragments into one,
the seagull circles, predator as prey—

while the white screen agitates:

     a diversity of gray.

2

Nevertheless, that your sanatorium still floats is proof
the projector's still running. As if made of glass,
you blew on it—exhalia—expected, of all things, weather.

Put a finger to the patchwork and rubbed. The extravagant sway.
As if to *see away* precluded falling through.
As if you have opened a new window into the body.

Let stand our long-standing long-screened
witness become, through continuance,
our dearest matinee, our vision of persistence.

The jagged shards of the ancient *as*, the shattered states
of bulb, shoreline's fractal,
the unsustainable elegiac
crisis. The new anxiety that says:

It is your absence of luminescence that lures me to you.

Piece by piece you let me in.

3

"Plash"—the view itself consumes,
presupposes the death of the viewer who scened it.
Having not been designed to handle the force

of splash, Pooled Projections, or Spool That is Projected,
or Plural Symmetries Projecting All but What Is.
Cinema of the Ineffable.
Only to be told: Dark collar, dark reel,
I will make my way to you.

I will swim to the left of your very dim shining.
I will swim to the right of your very dim shining.
Sky gull, gull sky, palindrome the old, the new.

Once syncretic, will it then be true or is it
mere mysticism of a benign schizophrenia,
the melting away of the bipolar films

that project onto each its dripping opposite
from the depths surfacing
to prey on the shape of you that remains still-you

—black glacier, dim shining—on which you, in turn,
will prey through me, my flesh, your vessel.
Fragment into one in the eyes
of above. You whom I love:

blend in with the sky.

Generation of bird,
who's singular vanishing's lasting syntax
spills from the littoral into open sea.

FURTHER ALONG NOW

If they are arriving or fleeing, if the tide is upon me, mining me for what I know of here and now, of worlds just out of reach. I could have sworn the blue of that which we explored was not a dream was not simply a dream that comes and goes. I've worried my mind, distilled my eyes into a visionary tonic, brave and astringent, that I forever apply, evenly, serenely, the way you deserve. Particular motions of southern seas, of northern seas, false sightings etched into the backs of eyelids, to permeate our dreams, to become signposts in our dreams, to become the repeated words of our dreams, accumulating and breaking free like landslides. How the firmest earth freely slides.

Further along the curves of gesture, the delicate apostrophe, in the tongue of muted suns, we'll find ourselves in a clearing, in a meadow of ancient grass, picking apart what has long been picked apart. Further along, the compliments, the tweezers and logic, the laboratory of hard hats and felt pens and hard heads and clipboards hanging from sky's bloody fender, bird droppings steaming calligraphic so long as the clouds become clouds become clouds and amazed we see in such preventable warfare our own substances unchanging. Fountains of ash too diffuse to interpret, too complex to diagnose, I quote the many woods of grief, too far alone, too deep.

I have been taking on the dewdrops of ages, antiquity's
shine beading down the byline, the interstate that moves me back
and forth through psyches no longer my own, to background's
girders, foreground's girdles of murderous hips of murderous
breasts, of collective mist in a jar on a schoolchild's desk. In the
drawer is always another drawer worth exploring. A light bulb at
rest on the gravel road.

My sweet felony, my emphatic and empathic laborer of shine. That we both fall in our dreams is a harmony just out of reach, is a harmony proved by our shared loose teeth, by our inability to sprint in our morning sleep. Our drift of drowsy innocents a singular web of what in us is most revelatory, most human, most fundamentally felon. The new anxiety says that what we know of ourselves we're sold by the world, our shiest finch. The prettiest buyers. Generations of bird, which follow follow follow, in water washed away—my canoe is filled with your feathers.

Mingled as they were with former versions of themselves, tarnished to a fleeting image of an endless waving, first goodbye, then goodbye, a scullery by way of broken promise, limp handshake on the esplanade, the dish rack, a red striped suit, your umbrella dimple, the puddles that adorn me in my shaggle netherhood, how I heard you bemoan your own dreams, your own omen-stick in aquarium light, the fountain of missed markings, of sightings blurred and gone to black. I have blurred and gone to black. I have been pointed at, pressed the button at, yet my light's burned bad, screen's blue-struck intuit, some incendiary after-mode, corpse of firefly in smear, behind the eyes, bakelight, my Fender oven, my kitchen madness stilting down cellar steps, brandishing a last-century idea, a genuine endeavor worth exploring by means of hunkering down further along the shore in a garden of black petals. To become a garden of black petals.

Where the shoreline salt meets the filmic body, both endless effluence and compression flicker. I lost what it was made me afraid of losing you.

Further along now, the sightings of planets over the horizon, the collective gasp, the eyes have all stopped blinking. Naiveté has turned on itself, has hardened. On shore, a series of caulking guns, a garden of bronze petals greeting one another with shoulder caresses. Glue the fleck storm, place a touchable screen, touch it. I'll stretch your canvas there, ache for a more distant frame, unearthed at intervals in a timely fashion, geometrically sane. I am geometrically sane. I am full of horizons glinting for you, I have sleeves of mirages bursting for you, something worth carrying over. Something worth holding here.

ROCK CREEK, PRE-DAWN

Natural history is the gentleness with which she placed
her arms through her shirt-sleeves. The faces
on the refrigerator newly dusted,
the lettuce wilted, wet timberline and brow. Mistrusted
fluids of the plastic sack. In this present, I fight
it precisely, twist and tear filled pockets. I am, unlike
my predecessor, entirely anxious when I awake to twilight,
an afternoon nap, feet beyond the edge of the sheet.
Autumn is upon me once again, and I sweep
the walls of nymphal skins,
of stonefly youths, small recognitions.
It was the gentleness with which she teethed,
broke free. Naturally, historically,
my dreams of late issue domestic truths
that gnaw my wrists to transformative raw.
I can awake to these soft hours of truce
no more. Misgivings and bruises.
I conjure the sound of the creek though I must
undress in the silence of recurring light.

ROCK CREEK, PRE-DAWN

Ineluctable these reflections of the stars in the creek,
mid-day, when the radiance that's said to take seven years to arrive
is welcomed prematurely, is in time for aperitifs.
The darting white fish boldly rise,
mistaking stars for mayflies, swarm & frenzy.
I have seen you in various stages of undress, I'm chanting,
when the shooting star strikes across the lake like a match.
& that is when it happens: my desire
tears through the surface of each posthistoric sea,
its vast mouth an empty stairwell, dark and deep,
in which you, poised in white lab coat,
cradle a jar overflowing,
storm of blue bees. Eternal specimen
of the eyes I have for you.

NOTES

"We Are All of Us Nearly Home" is for Joanna Klink.

"The Last Arctic" owes its structure, as well as a few key lines, to Lucie Brock-Broido's poem "Birdie Africa."

"Stitches" is for Marc T. Wise.

"The Dual-Shade of Six-Prong" is for my brothers, Thomas and Nicholas.

"Logic of Rawhide" is indebted to Frank Stanford's "Blue Yodel of the Desperado."

The epigraph in "Translations of 'My Refrigerator Light Makes Its Way Toward You' . . ." is adapted from Franz Wright's line *"Man was born / when an animal wept."*

"Biography of Creek" owes its existence to Richard Meier's "Biography of Grass" and Wallace Stevens's "Anecdote of the Jar."

"Her Hunger, Barometrical" is for Greg Hill Jr.

"Whensoever It Snows, My Vermont," "Further Along Now," and "Rock Creek, Pre-Dawn [II] are for Louisa Conrad.

"Rock Creek, Pre-Dawn [II]" cribbed the line *"I have seen you in various stages of undress"* from a song ("Various Stages") by the Great Lake Swimmers.

ACKNOWLEDGMENTS

Thank you to the editors of the following publications in which some of these poems first appeared, occasionally in different form:

Alice Blue, Boston Review, Cannibal, The Equalizer, Eucalyptus: A Journal of the Broken Narrative, Forklift, Ohio, Greatcoat Magazine, Handsome, Inknode, Jubilat, Le Petite Zine, NEO, No Tell Motel, Slope, Strange Machine, and Upstairs at Duroc.

Thank you to Amanda Raczkowski and Joseph Reed at Caketrain Press for originally publishing some of these poems in a chapbook titled *Bird Any Damn Kind* (Caketrain, 2010).

"Geosmin" was selected as winner of a 2008 Academy of American Poets College & University Prize.

"Translations of 'My Refrigerator Light Makes Its Way Toward You' into the 34 Languages Spoken in the Many Woods of Grief" (originally published by *Alice Blue*) was selected for inclusion in Dzanc Books' *Best of the Web 2010*.

Many thanks to those who provided guidance or otherwise helped inspire this book's creation: Thomas Arthur Farrell, Nicholas Farrell, Ethan Paquin, Brandon Shimoda, Greg Hill Jr., Elisabeth Benjamin, Karen Volkman, Greg Pape, Robert Baker, Daniel Whitmore, and Marc T. Wise. Thank you to my parents, Thomas and Deborah Farrell, for their infinite love and support. Thank you to Doris Ekstrom, my muse at Rock Creek. Thank you to the Vermont Studio Center. A tremendous and everlasting thank you to Dara Wier, James Tate, and James Haug at the University of Massachusetts. As well as Bruce Wilcox, Carol Betsch, and Sally Nichols. Thank you to all my former classmates, teachers, and friends at the University of Montana, especially Matthew Kaler, Catherine Moore, and Youna Kwak. An enormous thank you to Joanna Klink—my dear mentor and friend. Finally, as ever, my abiding love and gratitude to Louisa Conrad: laborer of shine.

The Juniper Prize

This volume is the 35th recipient of the
Juniper Prize for Poetry presented annually by the
University of Massachusetts Press for a volume of
original poetry. The prize is named in honor of
Robert Francis (1901–1987), who lived for many years
at Fort Juniper, Amherst, Massachusetts.